SQUISH

Blush

WHAT'S WRONG? ARE YOU AFRAID SOMEONE WILL SEE US?

AWW!

HMM...

SHOVE

YES!

EXACTLY!

SAY WHAT YOU WANT, KOUTA-KUN...

Boing

WE'RE OUTSIDE! IN THE DAYTIME! AND WE'RE NEAR THE SCHOOL!!

WHAT ARE YOU THINKING?

Y-YOU CAN'T FLASH YOUR PANTIES IN PUBLIC!

I'M SORRY, KOUTA-KUN.

OH!

Grab

OH MY...

AH!

MMM...

GASP!

BA-THUMP

BA-THUMP

KOUTA-KUN, YOU JERK!

sizzle

sizzle

sizzle!!

......

PHEW!

WAG

THANKS TO THAT MANEUVER, I'M SAFE FOR NOW.

OF COURSE I AM!

A-ARE YOU MAD?

WE CONFESSED OUR LOVE TO EACH OTHER... EVERYONE KNOWS THAT THE NEXT BIG STEP FOR A COUPLE IS TO...

WHY DID YOU DO THAT?!

I'M SORRY.

I'M SORRY FOR PUSHING YOU, KOUTA-KUN.

I GOT TOO EXCITED.

WE SHOULDN'T RUSH THINGS. I WANT OUR FIRST TIME TO BE SPECIAL. I WANT IT TO BE MORE THAN A QUICKIE IN THE STREET.

Y-YEAH...

WHY ARE YOU SO EAGER TO, UH, "DO IT"?

CHIZURU-SAN...

UM...

LET'S SEE...

SEE YA LATER, LOVER!

I NEED TO GO BUY THE MATERIALS!

Dash dash

HERE WE ARE!

100 WAYS TO EXCITE YOUR OBLIVIOUS BOYFRIEND

WELL, NO TIME LIKE THE PRESENT!

. . . . .

"OBLIVIOUS BOYFRIEND"? WHAT ARE THEY *TALKING* ABOUT?

Ezomori Nozomu

■■■■■■■■■■■■■■■■■

This is the silver-haired (hehehe!) Nozomu. Sorry, the one giggling is me, not Nozomu. I mean, all of the characters up until now have had black hair...

It would be a spoiler if I told you her backstory now, so I'll just add it to Saku's character page later in the book. No peeking!

■■■■■■■■■■■■■■■

Ezomori Nozomu

CHAPTER 7

I've Already Memorized Your Scent

I'M NOZOMU.

EZOMORI NOZOMU.

EZOMORI NOZOMU.. THE NAME DOESN'T RING A BELL...

JUDGING BY THE COLOR OF HER SCHOOL CREST SHE MUST BE A FIRST-YEAR STUDENT LIKE ME. BUT I'M SURE I'VE NEVER SEEN HER BEFORE...

EZO-MORI...?

NOZOMU.

SOMEBODY'S GOT TO PICK UP HER TAB.

HUH?

SO THEN WHY...?

DO YOU KNOW THIS GIRL?

BE A PAL AND PAY FOR YOUR GIRLFRIEND'S MEAL.

?

SHE'S NOT MY--!

NO, NO! YOU'VE GOT IT ALL WRONG!

Toss

HEY...! FOR GOD'S SAKE, STOP EATING!

I CAN'T RUN A BUSINESS THIS WAY! WHENEVER I ASK HER TO PAY UP, SHE DOESN'T ANSWER...

HOLY COW. THAT'S A LOT OF FOOD...

Pile o' Bones

UH... D-DON'T WORRY!

BUT, EVEN THEN...

Grab

Grab

THAT'S WHY...

CHIZURU-SAN, I...

KOUTA-KUN--

AHEM!

NO MATTER THE EXCUSE, MAKING A GIRL CRY IS WRONG.

KOUTA-KUN...?

Fun fact: These two actually debuted back in volume 1.

Yooks' family is loaded (one of her parents is a doctor), so she has a lot of expensive gadgets on her all the time. Kii-chan (who comes from a less well-off family) is more likely to reflect the general opinion of the student body (especially in regards to Kouta).

Sasamori Yuuki (Yooks)

Sasamori Yuuki & Takana Kiriko

Takana Kiriko (Kii-chan)

It may seem like Kii-chan is just being strung along by Yooks, but they really are good friends. If you want to learn more about them, read the fourth volume of the light novel series!

HUH?

EZOMORI? THAT CAN'T BE...

AH, ANOTHER DAY, ANOTHER LECTURE FROM THE CLASS REP, EH, CHIZURU? WHAT IS IT THIS TIME--

HOLY CRAP, YOU HAVE ANOTHER GIRL ON THE SIDE?! *THATTABOY!* DON'T STOP! KEEP PLAYING THE FIELD!

Eek!

SHUT UP!!

IS SHE ALSO YOURS?

MINE?!

HEY, KOUTA...

WHAT? *WHY?!* I GET CHIZURU, BUT ASAHINA TOO?

THAT GUY'S GOOD.

OH?

GRR! WHEN I FINISH THIS GUY, I KILL YOU NEXT!

DON'T WORRY, BRAT. I HAVE ABSOLUTELY NO DESIRE TO HELP YOU.

THIS FIGHT'S ALREADY OVER.

KIRIYAMA DIDN'T EVEN LOOK OVER AT US...

HE CAN'T LET HIS GUARD DOWN FOR A SECOND. IF HE GIVES THAT GUY EVEN ONE OPENING, THIS FIGHT'S OVER.

HUH? *YOU* KNOW DOGGY TOO, KOUTA-KUN?

D-DOGGY?

DO YOU KNOW HIM?

CHI-ZURU-SAN...

EVEN KUMADA COULDN'T HANDLE *HIM*...

WHOOSH

GRR...

BLAM

ARGGH!

AH!

Phew!

LET'S CALL IT A DAY, KID.

drop

*ANISAMA: NOZOMU HAS A PECULIAR WAY OF SAYING "OLDER BROTHER." ON ONE SIDE, IT'S VERY INFORMAL AS ONE DOES NOT USUALLY REFER TO A BROTHER AS "ANI" DIRECTLY TO THEIR FACE. HOWEVER, SHE ALSO USES "-SAMA," WHICH INDICATES THE HIGHEST FORM OF POLITENESS.

Ezomori Saku

■■■■■■■■■■■■■■■

Saku was born on a moonless night, and, according to his hazy memory, that's why he decided to name himself "Saku" (an old word for "new moon").

Nozomu means full moon (the opposite of a new moon), so he named his sister that.

Every time I draw this cool, long-haired pretty boy, I have delusions that he might be a member of the Silver Saints from Saint·Seiya. He's a mentor to Nozomu, a Bronze Saint. Sahara-sensei is a Gold Saint.

I tried putting him in a school uniform, but it just didn't suit him...

■■■■■■■■■■■■■■

Ezomori
Saku

CHAPTER
8
He Knows a
Side of Her I
Don't Know
Part 2

IS ANYONE HURT?!

KA-RACK

NO? THEN GET TO CLASS!

OUR CLASS REP'S REALLY CRACKING THE WHIP.

EAN

YEAH, I'M FINE. I'VE BEEN HELPING ASAHINA WITH CROWD CONTROL. KIRIYAMA'S OKAY TOO.

TAYURA-KUN, ARE YOU ALL RIGHT?

FLAP FLAP

Dash

WE WERE JUST PART- NERS!!

DON'T SAY IT LIKE *THAT!*

BEFORE YOU, *I* WAS THE MAIN MAN IN HER LIFE. RIGHT, CHIZURU?

NOT AS IN LOVERS OR ANYTHING...

B-BUT NOT LIKE *THAT!*

LOV- ERS...?

PART- NERS...?

IT WASN'T LIKE THAT! HE WAS JUST A COMPANION!

COMP- ANION...?

Wobble

KOUTA- KUN!

RIGHT!

NOT HAPPENING. WE CAN'T GIVE OUT INFORMATION ABOUT INDIVIDUAL STUDENTS.

HE KNEW ABOUT KOUTA-KUN! AND SO DID HIS LITTLE SISTER!

SHOW ME EZOMORI SAKU'S FILE.

HMM, INTERESTING. EVEN IF HE DID SOME INVESTIGATING INTO MINAMOTO-SAN, OTHER THINGS JUST DON'T ADD UP.

IN ORDER FOR YOKAI TO BE ADMITTED INTO THIS SCHOOL, THEY HAVE TO FIRST GO THROUGH AN EVALUATION PROCESS THAT TAKES TWO MONTHS.

EXACTLY! AND KOUTA-KUN AND I ONLY MET A MONTH AGO!

SO THEY COULDN'T HAVE KNOWN ABOUT US BEFORE DECIDING TO TRANSFER HERE! SO WHAT'S THEIR DEAL?!

YOU TWO LITERALLY BECAME ONE MIND AND BODY. OF *COURSE* YOU'D BE SERIOUS ABOUT EACH OTHER. I JUST DIDN'T REALIZE HOW MUCH.

HEY, YOU'RE DOING IT AGAIN! STOP ASKING ABOUT KOUTA-KUN!

SORRY!

I *DIDN'T* UNTIL NOW. WAS I RIGHT?

HE *KNOWS* CHIZURU-SAN CAN POSSESS ME?!

UM...

HOW DID YOU KNOW ABOUT...?

HM?

SORRY, NOZOMU. LOOKS LIKE KOUTA-KUN'S ALREADY DOING THE DIRTY WITH CHIZURU.

GAG

HERE'S OUR TRANSFER PAPERS.

WHY DOESN'T IT BOTHER YOU?!

IT DOESN'T BOTHER ME.

SO WHAT?

INDEED.

シュルルーoo
shift

シュルルル
shift

. . . . . .

SHUT UP, HAG!!

SO, IS HE CORRECT? ARE YOU TWO ENGAGING IN SEXUAL ACTIVITIES?

YOU EVEN KNOW ABOUT THAT?

MY MY! SO *YOU'RE* SUPERVISOR SAHARA. OR RATHER, THE YOKAI INSIDE OF YOU IS...

MINAMOTO, WATCH YOUR MOUTH! THAT'S NO WAY TO SPEAK TO THE BOSS!

WHO ARE YOU REALLY?

SOMEHOW I DOUBT THAT, YOUNG MAN. WHAT ARE YOU UP TO?

I'M JUST YOUR RUN-OF-THE-MILL WOLF!

I DO HAVE AN ULTERIOR MOTIVE FOR COMING HERE.

WELL, NOW THAT THE BOSS IS HERE I MAY AS WELL COME CLEAN...

DEFEAT THE STRONG- EST YOKAI IN THIS SCHOOL.

AFTER THAT, THE YOKAI WING OF THIS SCHOOL WILL SIMPLY FALL APART ON ITS OWN...

SLIDE

Pass

AS FOR ME...

ANISAMA WANTS TO DESTROY THIS PLACE.

AS IF I'LL LET HIM!

KUNPU

BUT I DON'T SAY "WAN."

KAWAOON

KANOKON

"KANOWAN" HAS A BETTER RING TO IT THAN "KANOWAOON."

THAT'S TRUE.

BUT IT *DOES* SOUNDS LIKE *MATSUKEN*...

NO IT DOESN'T...

WE DON'T REALLY SAY "KON" THAT MUCH EITHER. IT SOUNDS MORE LIKE "KEEN." LET'S CHANGE IT TO KANOKEN.

NO WAY! THAT'S NOT CUTE AT ALL!

KEN

*MATSUKEN IS THE NICKNAME OF POPULAR JAPANESE ACTOR KEN MATSUDAIRA.

...UH...K-KON-IRO NO YUUWAKU (NAVY BLUE SEDUCTION)...?

KONBATIRAA V! (COMBATTLER V!)

KONBIIFU! (CORNED BEEF!)

I'VE BEEN WONDERING THIS FOR A WHILE, BUT WHAT DOES *KANOKON* MEAN?

I GET THAT "KANO" IS FOR "KANOJO" (GIRLFRIEND), BUT WHY ADD "KON" AT THE END?

HA HA HA!

VROOM...

"COUGHED"? CHIZURU-SAN LOOKS HEALTHY TO ME...

IT'S THE "KON" IN "KANOJO WA KON TO, KOWAIKU SEKI WO SHITE" ("SHE COUGHED WITH A CUTE LITTLE 'YIP'"), THE TITLE USED BY THE ORIGINAL AUTHOR NISHINO-SENSEI WHEN HE SUBMITTED IT TO THE NEW TALENT AWARDS.

CHAPTER 9

I Am (We Are) Trying Our Hardest
Part 1

EZO-MORI-SAN.

YOU CAN'T CLING TO OYAMADA-KUN LIKE THAT. YOU NEED TO SIT IN YOUR OWN SEAT.

BUT...

HEY, I'M *RIGHT HERE,* YOU KNOW...

Hmm...

LOOK, OYAMADA-KUN IS A BIT OF A NAIVE IDIOT, SO IF YOU KEEP ACTING LIKE THIS YOU'RE JUST GOING TO SCARE HIM OFF.

SHE SAID I'D LEARN HOW STRONG MY ENEMY WAS BY SEEING IF SHE FELT COMFORTABLE TELLING ME THE TRUTH OR NOT.

SHE SAID I SHOULD JUST ASK CHIZURU ABOUT KOUTA'S FAVORITE THINGS.

AKANE SAID "KNOW YOUR ENEMY, KNOW YOURSELF, AND YOU SHALL NOT FEAR A HUNDRED BATTLES."

JEEZ, ASAHINA... GOD HELP ME IF I EVER GET ON YOUR BAD SIDE...

"AKANE"? ASAHINA SAID THAT?

BUY THIS.

Monthly Media Victoria
"Peace," December Edition

BUT IF THIS GIRL *WERE* TO HOOK UP WITH KOUTA, IT MIGHT WORK OUT WELL FOR ME...

SPIN

OKAY, LISTEN UP!

CHIZURU'S USING IT AS A GUIDE TO WIN KOUTA OVER. BUY IT AND YOU'LL KNOW HER WHOLE GAME PLAN.

IT'S A WOMAN'S MAGAZINE.

HOW DID YOU KNOW IT WAS ME? MY TAYURA TRANSFORMATION WAS FLAWLESS AND YOU *STILL* SPOTTED ME!

KOUTA-KUN!

T-TRANS-FOR-MED?

WHY?

...

squish

HEHE! COULD IT BE THE POWER OF LOVE?

UMPF!

WELL, BE-CAUSE...

HEY...

CHIZURU.

UH...

THEN...

YOU DON'T NEED A "-SAN" AFTER NOZOMU.

...NO-ZOMU-CHAN?

SHOCK

CHI-ZURU-CHAN?

THAT'S NOT FAIR! CALL ME CHIZURU-CHAN!

WHAT GIVES?! YOU STILL CALL ME CHIZURU-SAN!!

RAA'AWR!

JUDO'S FUN! LET'S GRAPPLE, KOUTA-KUN! I'M SO GLAD BOYS AND GIRLS HAVE SEPARATE GYM CLASSES!!

DASH

UM, CHIZURU-SAN...

BE CAREFUL, CHIZURU-SAN! THE OTHERS WILL BE OUT OF THE LOCKER ROOM ANY MINUTE NOW!

DASH

OKAY!

PLEASE WEAR A T-SHIRT UNDER YOUR UNIFORM...

BOUNCE

BOUNCE

I KNOW, B-B-BUT...

WHY? YOU'RE NOT WEARING ONE.

ず"""SLAM ん、

HE FOUND TAYURA ALONG THE WAY AND FIGURED IT ALL OUT.

YATSUKA-SENSEI CARRIED YOU TO THE CLINIC.

CHIZURU-SAN, ARE YOU ALL RIGHT?

KOUTA-KUN...

ARE YOU MAD?

Grip

THAT'S WHAT *I* WANTED TO ASK *YOU*. I WAS CONCERNED WHEN I HEARD THAT MY FAVORITE CLASSMATE WAS OUT SICK, BUT THEN I LEARNED YOU WERE AT SCHOOL AFTER ALL.

SAKU! WHAT ARE YOU DOING HERE?!

YEAH. YESTERDAY I JUST INTRODUCED MYSELF TO THE HOMEROOM CLASS AND LEFT, SO I GUESS YOU MISSED THAT.

WHAT?! THEY PUT YOU IN MY CLASS?!

SAKU, WAIT!

WELL, I'M GLAD YOU'RE ALL RIGHT. SEE YA.

WHAT'S UP? I'M SKIPPING OUT EARLY, SO DON'T GO TATTLING ON ME.

I TOLD YOU. THE DESTRUCTION OF KUNPU ACADEMY.

CALL IT MY PET PROJECT.

WHAT'S SO IMPORTANT THAT YOU'RE CUTTING CLASS?

WHEN NOZOMU FIRST MET KOUTA-KUN, HE KNEW THAT SHE WAS REALLY A YOKAI.

WH-WHA...?

AND YESTERDAY HE DODGED THE AIR BLADE THAT WEASEL KID THREW...

EVEN THOUGH IT SHOULDN'T HAVE BEEN VISIBLE TO HUMAN EYES.

Whoosh

WELL, IN MY OPINION...

NOW THAT YOU MENTION IT...

I THOUGHT IT MIGHT BE BECAUSE YOU TWO HAD BEEN MERGING TOO MUCH.

HE WAS ABLE TO SEE THROUGH MY TRANSFORMATION TODAY WITH ONE GLANCE. AND BEFORE THAT... HE FORCED ME TO POSSESS HIM.

I REALLY DO HAVE SOME.

Yet again, I got the story for this bonus manga
from the original creator, Nishino-sensei.
Thank you so much!

You know, it came as a shock to have Nozomu
eating carbs.

This was the first time I showed her eating
something other than meat. Once she realized
there are good things to eat besides meat, she
started to eat vegetables. The end. (Not really.)

I hope we can meet again in volume 4!

RIN YAMAKI

DAMN IT!

WHO DOES THAT DUMB WOLF *THINK* HE IS?!

YOU'VE GOT TO BE *JOKING!*

I HAVEN'T SEEN HIM IN YEARS AND NOW ALL HE WANTS TO DO IS *DESTROY THE SCHOOL?!*

THIS MUST BE KARMA GETTING ME BACK FOR BEING SO BEAUTIFUL! THIS SCHOOL WAS MY LAST CHANCE! WITHOUT IT I'D BE LOCKED UP!!

AND IF THAT HAPPENS... *NOOO!* I'LL BE NEVER SEE KOUTA-KUN AGAIN!

WAHHH!

BUT...

EXTRA

Afterschool Yokai ~Nozomu's Story~

CHAPTER **9**

I Am (We Are)
Trying Our
Hardest
Part 2

M-MAYBE BECAUSE SHE'S ALMOST NAKED?

EITHER WAY, IT'S GETTING HARDER AND HARDER TO SAY NO...

thk
Plunk

OR BECAUSE SHE'S WRAPPED TIGHTLY IN A BATH TOWEL?

SOON I MIGHT...!

I WON'T DO ANYTHING.

I PROMISE...

I JUST WANT TO JOIN YOU IN THE BATH.

OR BECAUSE THE TOWEL IS WET?

DO YOU LIKE KIRIYAMA?

MIO...

WHAT?!

BUT ALL I CAN DO FOR HIM IS HEAL INJURIES WITH MY OIL...

BLUSH

Y-YES...

UM, UM, UM...

YUP.

You did come from the bathhouse just now...

D-DON'T TELL ME THAT YOU ACTUALLY TRIED THAT...

WHILE WE WERE FIGHTING, KOUTA CAME TO. BUT THEN HE LOST EVEN MORE BLOOD...

BEFORE WE COULD HELP HIM, HE GRABBED HIS CLOTHES AND RAN BACK TO HIS ROOM, SCREAMING.

M-MAYBE HE WAS AFRAID YOUR "HELP" WOULD MAKE THINGS WORSE...

Spurt

CHIZURU AND I FOUGHT OVER WHO GOT TO GIVE HIM CPR.

CHI-ZURU-SAN WAS THERE TOO?

KOUTA GOT A HUGE NOSEBLEED AND WENT ALL FLOATY.

IT'S EASY TO SCARE A NAÏVE IDIOT LIKE KOUTA!

OH, THAT'S TRUE!

ALSO, I WAS INVITED TO JOIN THE SCHOOL'S YOKAI CLUB.

YOU DON'T SAY!

I TOOK A BATH WITH KOUTA AND CHIZURU.

REALLY? ARE YOU GOING TO JOIN?

NO.

YOU SAID BEFORE THAT YOU WERE A LONE WOLF, ANISAMA.

I'M A LONE WOLF, TOO.

THAT'S NICE. TOO BAD YOU CAN'T SPEND MORE TIME WITH THEM.

HA HA HA!

YUP! THEY'RE ALL GOOD PEOPLE.

WHAT?

NOZO-MU...

THERE'S ONLY A WEEK LEFT.

BUT WE WERE GOING TO GO TO THE HOT SPRINGS...

THIS SCHOOL IS EVEN WEAKER THAN I THOUGHT IT WAS. I'M ALMOST DONE WITH MY RESEARCH, AND THEN I'LL BE FINISHED HERE.

THEN...

YES...
INDEED
YOU ARE.

HALF
RIGHT?

THAT'S
ALL I
CAN
SAY
FOR
NOW.

BUT
ONLY
HALF
RIGHT.

THE
WALLS HAVE
EARS HERE--
YOU SHOULD
KNOW. JUST
THE OTHER
DAY SOMEONE
LISTENED
IN ON YOUR
CONVERSATION
WITH
MINAMOTO,
CORRECT?

I WAS
CARELESS.
IT WON'T
HAPPEN
AGAIN.

TO CELEBRATE THE NEW *KANOKON* ANIME,
I WAS SHOWN SOME OF THE DESIGNS AND
MATERIALS FOR THE SHOW. I EVEN SAW
ALL THE LITTLE DETAILS LIKE THE
BLUEPRINTS OF THE SCHOOL, THE DESIGNS
OF EACH OF THE ROOMS, AND THE
STUDENTS' HANDBAGS. I WAS A LITTLE
INTIMIDATED BY ALL THE DETAIL! I KNOW
IT'S A BIT LATE, BUT THE DESIGNS FOR
THE MANGA VERSION ARE READY!
ALTHOUGH IT'S NOT VERY MUCH...

IN COMMEMORATION OF
THE *KANOKON* ANIME:
祝☆かのこんアニメ化記念
漫画版設定資料公開!
INITIAL MANGA DESIGNS UNVEILED!

FIRST, A CHARACTER COMPARISON DIAGRAM.
THE NAMES GO IN ORDER OF HEIGHT WITH THE ONES
ON THE LEFT BEING THE TALLEST (GENERALLY).

ABOUT 184CM
SAKU - YATSUKA
TAYURA

ABOUT 156CM
NOZOMU - KIRIYAMA
SAHARA - KOUTA - AKANE

AS BIG AS
I DAMN WELL PLEASE
KUMADA

ABOUT 170CM
CHIZURU

ABOUT 142CM
MIO

THE DIFFERENCE OF 14 CENTIMETERS BETWEEN CHIZURU AND KOUTA
IS BECAUSE THAT'S HOW TALL SHE IS WHEN HER EARS ARE OUT!

WHEN I DRAW CHIZURU, I ALWAYS MEASURE THE DIFFERENCE IN
HEIGHT FROM AROUND THE HEIGHT OF HER EARS.

DON'T GET TOO EXCITED. IT'S JUST LEFTOVERS FROM SUPPER YESTERDAY.

AHHH!

WAIT...

SERI-OUSLY?!

I WAS SO WORRIED THAT IT DIDN'T TURN OUT WELL... HAVE MORE!

IT WAS SO TASTY HE SCREAMED! ♥

YEAH, I COULD, BUT...

YOU KNOW, YOU COULD JUST BUY A LUNCH ON YOUR WAY TO SCHOOL.

MMM! THIS IS REALLY GOOD!

GWAHHH!

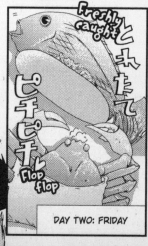

Freshly caught

Flop flop

DAY TWO: FRIDAY

ASAHINA MADE IT?!

AND MOM'S SICK WITH A COLD, SO SHE COULDN'T MAKE ANYTHING...

THEN THAT MEANS...

THERE WEREN'T A LOT OF LEFTOVERS LAST NIGHT...

Spicy!

GASP!

Y-YEAH. IT'S GREAT...

ARE YOU OKAY?

Mnch

WHAT?

M-MINA-MOTO!

ARE YOU...?!

がstand タ!!

BLUSH

chomp

HYPO-CRITE...

......!

BLUSH

AHHHHGH!

AHH...

THAT'S NOT WHAT I MEANT...

THEN YOU CAN KEEP THEM!

BUT THANKS TO *YOU*, I FEEL A LOT BETTER NOW, KOUTA-KUN!

IT FELT LIKE A BIG BALL OF STRESS WAS JUST BUILDING INSIDE ME...

THINGS HAVE BEEN KINDA ROUGH LATELY...

"KINDA ROUGH LATELY"...?

ARE YOU TALKING ABOUT NOZOMU'S BROTHER COMING HERE?

I'LL PROTECT YOU.

DON'T WORRY, KOUTA-KUN. NO MATTER WHAT HE'S UP TO...

I'LL PROTECT YOU AND THIS SCHOOL.

HERE.

slip

THIS IS AMAZING! I CAN'T BELIEVE YOU MADE IT YOURSELF.

I KNITTED IT FOR YOU.

WHO...

DO YOU THINK YOU'RE FOOLING?

squeeze

YOU KNOW, THANKS TO YOUR DUMB BROTHER, I'VE BEEN STAYING UP ALL NIGHT FOR DAYS!

I MADE IT. I STAYED UP ALL NIGHT TO FINISH IT.

NO WAY IS THAT HOMEMADE! IT'S TOO GOOD!

CHIZURU DID VISIT ANISAMA LAST NIGHT...

SO THERE REALLY *IS* SOMETHING GOING ON BETWEEN YOU AND SAKU-SAN!

WHAT?

Whoosh

Thud!

SHUT UP!

AND THE NIGHT BEFORE THAT, AND THE NIGHT BEFORE THAT, AND THE NIGHT BEFORE--

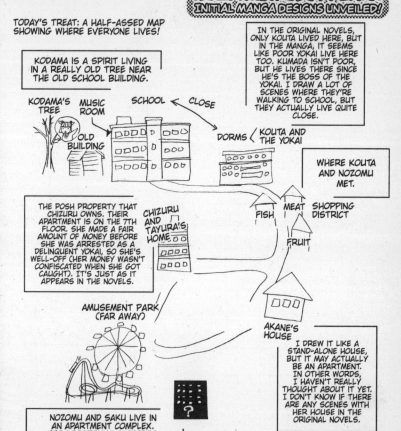

TODAY'S TREAT: A HALF-ASSED MAP SHOWING WHERE EVERYONE LIVES!

KODAMA IS A SPIRIT LIVING IN A REALLY OLD TREE NEAR THE OLD SCHOOL BUILDING.

IN THE ORIGINAL NOVELS, ONLY KOUTA LIVED HERE, BUT IN THE MANGA, IT SEEMS LIKE POOR YOKAI LIVE HERE TOO. KUMADA ISN'T POOR, BUT HE LIVES THERE SINCE HE'S THE BOSS OF THE YOKAI. I DRAW A LOT OF SCENES WHERE THEY'RE WALKING TO SCHOOL, BUT THEY ACTUALLY LIVE QUITE CLOSE.

KODAMA'S TREE — MUSIC ROOM

SCHOOL ← CLOSE

OLD BUILDING

DORMS 〈 KOUTA AND THE YOKAI

WHERE KOUTA AND NOZOMU MET.

THE POSH PROPERTY THAT CHIZURU OWNS. THEIR APARTMENT IS ON THE 7TH FLOOR. SHE MADE A FAIR AMOUNT OF MONEY BEFORE SHE WAS ARRESTED AS A DELINQUENT YOKAI, SO SHE'S WELL-OFF (HER MONEY WASN'T CONFISCATED WHEN SHE GOT CAUGHT). IT'S JUST AS IT APPEARS IN THE NOVELS.

CHIZURU AND TAYURA'S HOME

FISH | MEAT — SHOPPING DISTRICT

FRUIT

AMUSEMENT PARK (FAR AWAY)

AKANE'S HOUSE

I DREW IT LIKE A STAND-ALONE HOUSE, BUT IT MAY ACTUALLY BE AN APARTMENT. IN OTHER WORDS, I HAVEN'T REALLY THOUGHT ABOUT IT YET. I DON'T KNOW IF THERE ARE ANY SCENES WITH HER HOUSE IN THE ORIGINAL NOVELS.

NOZOMU AND SAKU LIVE IN AN APARTMENT COMPLEX. ITS LOCATION IS A SECRET.

I'VE RUN OUT OF LOCATIONS TO WRITE ABOUT, SO I'LL END IT HERE. AS ONE LAST THING, I'LL DRAW THUMBNAILS OF THE CHARACTERS. TO TELL THE TRUTH, THIS IS PRETTY MUCH ALL I HAVE AS FAR AS PLANNING FOR THE MANGA GOES... BUT THINGS WILL WORK OUT... RIGHT? I PROMISE I'LL WORK HARDER IN THE FUTURE.

HEH. NICE HIT...

I CAN SEE HOW YOU GAVE CHIZURU A RUN FOR HER MONEY...

HEHE! YOU'RE NOT HALF BAD YOURSELF!

THIS IS THE MOST REVVED UP I'VE BEEN SINCE I FOUGHT MINAMOTO!

I YIELD!

NO WONDER THE HIGHER-UPS ARE SO WARY.

SO MANY YOKAI, ALL IN ONE PLACE...

WELL, WELL...

IF THOSE YOKAI WERE LED BY A STRONG LEADER, THEY'D BE A FORCE TO BE RECKONED WITH.

A STRONG LEADER... LIKE KUMADA OR SAHARA...

OR EVEN... HER.

UM, JUST A SECOND...

THE ONLY REASON YOU CALLED KUMADA OUT WAS TO ASK *THAT!*

"IS OYAMADA KOUTA STRONGER THAN YOU WHEN HE'S POSSESSED BY CHIZURU?"

I TOLD YOU, DIDN'T I? MY PLAN IS TO DEFEAT THE STRONGEST YOKAI IN THE SCHOOL.

KUMADA ACKNOWLEDGES THAT YOU'RE STRONGER THAN HE IS...

SO THEN...

THAT'S RIGHT!

Lean

THE REASON I MADE NOZOMU APPROACH HIM, THE REASON I TOLD SAHARA AND YATSUKA ALL THAT CRAP ABOUT DESTROYING THE SCHOOL, THE REASON I FOUGHT WITH RYUUSEI KUMADA...

ALL OF IT WAS ALL TO LEARN WHAT KIND OF GUY OYAMADA KOUTA IS.

THE ONE I'M TRULY AFTER IS KOUTA-KUN.

AND *WHAT* DO YOU HOPE TO GAIN BY LEARNING THAT?

HMM. SHOULD I REALLY TELL YOU?

Froooo

NOZOMU-SAN...

I NEED TO TALK TO YOU ABOUT SOMETHING.

I'M SORRY, BUT--

DON'T SAY IT!

Grab

WHY?

PRETEND...?

I'VE ALWAYS FELT THAT CHIZURU-SAN WAS OUT OF MY LEAGUE...

SO I DIDN'T WANT HER TO KNOW HOW JEALOUS I WAS.

I DIDN'T WANT TO LOOK BAD.

BUT SHE *LIKED* IT.

EVEN THOUGH I SAID I GOT ANGRY AT CHIZURU-SAN FOR *HER* BENEFIT... REALLY, I JUST SNAPPED.

NOZOMU...

Grab

KOUTA, FROM THE DAY I FIRST MET YOU, AND EVERY DAY SINCE THEN, I'VE--

I DIDN'T MEAN TO, BUT MY HEART JUST FELT SO TIGHT AND--

I CAN'T BELIEVE I ACTUALLY CRIED...

IT'S OKAY. I WAS CRYING TOO.

HEH. WE'RE A COUPLE OF IDIOTS, AREN'T WE?

THERE ARE SOME THINGS I NEED TO TELL YOU... ABOUT WHAT MY ANISAMA IS PLOTTING...

KOUTA...

ANISAMA WORKS FOR KUDZU LEAF, THE ONES RUNNING KUNPU ACADEMY FROM THE SHADOWS.

O-OKAY...

AND... THE REASON ANISAMA WORKS FOR THEM IS BECAUSE OF *ME.*

SINCE I WAS ON MY OWN, THEY DIDN'T KNOW WHAT TO DO WITH ME. SOME OF THEM WANTED TO KEEP ME IN YOKAI PRISON UNTIL I GREW UP.

BEFORE I MET HIM, I WAS A WOLF WITHOUT A PACK.

WHAT DO YOU MEAN?

THAT'S WHY ANISAMA HAS TO WORK FOR KUDZU LEAF, AT LEAST UNTIL I GROW UP.

HE SAID HE'D LOOK AFTER ME.

AND SAKU HELPED YOU?

BUT...

EVEN THOUGH ANISAMA IS DOING THIS FOR MY SAKE *NOW*...

THE REASON HE JOINED IN THE FIRST PLACE WAS BECAUSE OF A WOMAN.

A WOMAN?

YES... HE'D BEEN IN LOVE WITH HER FOR A VERY, VERY LONG TIME.

IN ORDER TO PROTECT HER, HE JOINED THE ORGANIZATION.

THIS WOMAN... COULD IT BE--?

IT'S A GOOD THING I SENT THE BRAT AFTER HER.

I DUNNO, BUT...

HEY, CHIZURU-SAN SEEMED TO BE IN A MUCH BETTER MOOD THIS AFTERNOON.

I WONDER WHAT HAPPENED?

WHAT? IT'S TRUE!

ACK!

NICE TO SEE THAT YOU'VE *FINALLY* GOTTEN OVER YOUR SISTER COMPLEX. I GUESS I SHOULD THANK OYAMADA-KUN FOR THAT.

WELL, MY SISTER *COULD* DO WORSE THAN HIM...

OYAMADA-KUN! WHAT'S GOING ON?

IT'S CHIZURU'S SPECIAL PROTECTIVE KNITWEAR!

JUST LIKE THIS ROPE, IT'S MADE WITH VIRGIN'S HAIR!

NOT ONLY IS IT MADE WITH LOVE, IT ALSO CONTAINS MY FUR...

WHAT? I'M AS PURE AS FRESHLY-FALLEN SNOW!

YOU MEAN YOURS?

AND HAIR FROM A MORE *INTIMATE* PLACE MEANS THE EFFECT IS EVEN STRONGER.

IT'S RUE! I... HINK.

WHAT'S WITH *THAT* LOOK?!

WE'LL SHOW HIM THE POWER OF OUR LOVE!

BAM!!

LET'S GO, KOUTA-KUN!

ALL RIGHT!

Froo!!

HERE!

OH DEAR...

RUSTLE

RUSTLE RUSTLE

IT SEEMS YOU LOSE A LOT OF POWER USING THE SCARF AS A MEDIUM INSTEAD OF DIRECTLY FUSING WITH CHIZURU.

THEN ALL I HAVE TO DO IS UNTIE IT!

AS LONG AS IT BINDS YOU, YOU CAN'T POSSESS HIM.

I TOLD YOU. THAT ROPE'S SPECIALLY MADE.

YOU THINK I'LL JUST STAND BY AND LET YOU?

tFooo

THWACK

WELL, WELL!

NOT BAD...

SHAKE...

NICE KICK, KIDDO.

I'M JUST FOLLOWING MY OWN RULES.

IS THIS SOME REBELLIOUS TEENAGE STAGE? WHAT HAPPENED TO MY CUTE LITTLE SISTER?

BUT REALLY, NOZOMU, WHAT WERE YOU THINKING?

IF SOMEONE HURTS KOUTA, I'LL FIGHT THEM. EVEN IF THAT PERSON IS YOU, ANISAMA.

I LOVE KOUTA.

I KNOW YOU CAN FEND FOR YOURSELF, ANISAMA.

REALLY? YOU WOULDN'T HELP ME?

KOUTA!

KOUTA-KUN!

!

Whack

RUN!

IT SEEMS KOUTA-KUN'S TOO NAIVE TO ACCEPT THAT.

PAT

IF YOU WANT TO PROTECT THE ONES YOU LOVE, YOU MUST BE WILLING TO DO *ANYTHING.* EVEN IF THAT MEANS GETTING YOUR HANDS DIRTY.

PAT

AT LEAST *YOU'VE* GOT YOUR PRIORITIES STRAIGHT, TAYURA.

LOOKS LIKE I HAVE NO CHOICE. KOUTA, IT'S TIME...

Clen

IF SAKU USES HIS TRUMP CARD...

HE LOSES ALL CONTROL!

TO PUSH YOUR LIMITS.

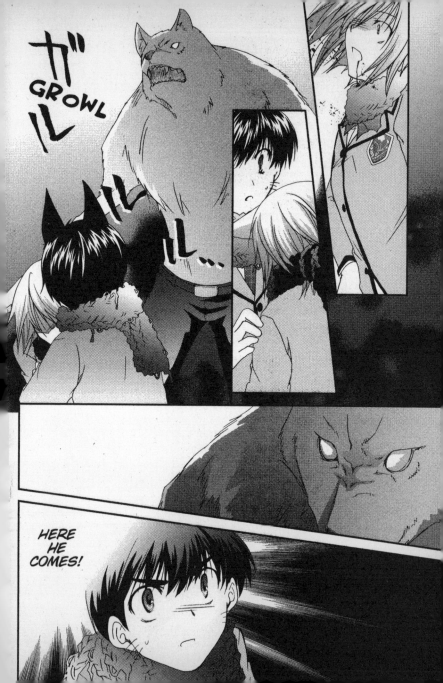

MIO...

HAS CRACKED.

EXTRA

Afterschool
Yokai
~Mio's
Story~

mutter

mutter

THE YOKAI AT THE SCHOOL SEARCHED THE NEARBY MOUNTAINS, BUT THERE WAS NO SIGN OF THE IDIOT.

IT'S BEEN A WEEK SINCE KIRIYAMA LEFT SAYING, "I TRAIN IN MOUNTAINS UNTIL I CAN BEAT SAKU."

WAH...

mutter

mutter

KIRIYAMA-KUUN!

OSAKABE'S LOST IT!

HERE IT IS!

DASH

SO THAT'S THE SITUA- TION...

CAN YOU GIVE HER SOME ADVICE? PLEASE?

SOB る

SOB る

SOB る

SOB |

SOB |

SOB |

ASTRO!

THANKS, KODAMA!

Umm okay...

AN OFFERING

KIRI-YAMA-KUUUN!

WAIT... IT WAS JUST A JOKE...

KIRI-YAMA-KUN?! WHERE IS HE?!

WHERE?!

OH, THERE'S KIRIYAMA!

JUMP

JUST CALM DOWN!

WHA?!

KODAMA BEAM
こだまびーむ

SINCE KODAMA IS A FOREST SPIRIT, SHE CAN MAKE HOLES IN THE GROUND ANYTIME SHE WANTS! IT'S PRETTY AMAZING!

ずぼーん
SWOOSH

I J-JUST DON'T KNOW WHAT TO DO...

KIRIYAMA-KUN D-D-DISAPPEARED AND EVERYONE SEARCHED THE M-MOUNTAINS, B-BUT WE COULDN'T FIND HIM ANYWHERE...

Sniff

Sniff

HMM.

TELL YOU WHAT, I'LL DO A FORTUNE READING FOR YOU.

YOU REALLY THINK KIRIYAMA-KUN'S ALL RIGHT?

WHO KNOWS?

Y-Y-YOU... YOU THINK SO?

KODAMA-MA-MA-MA...

F-FORTUNE READING?

So bring me more offerings!

SINCE KODAMA IS A FOREST SPIRIT, SHE CAN ALSO DO FORTUNE-TELLING! IT'S PRETTY AMAZING!

Amazing!

Afterword

HELLO. I'M YAMAKI RIN!

THANK YOU FOR BUYING KANOKON VOLUME 4!

I'LL GO AHEAD AND START WITH A QUESTION FROM A RELATIVE OF MINE.

LET'S SEE..."WHY DON'T YOU DO PANTY SHOTS OF NOZUMU? DO YOU LIKE HER LESS THAN THE OTHER GIRLS?"

ME?

OBVIOUSLY, IT'S BECAUSE READERS GET ENOUGH PANTY SHOTS FROM ME! ♡

MAYBE PEOPLE ARE TIRED OF SEEING YOUR UNDERWEAR! NOZUMU-SAN, YOU DON'T NEED TO FLASH YOUR PANTIES ALL THE TIME LIKE CHIZURU.

YOU GET TOO MANY PANTY SHOTS, CHIZURU-SAN!

WHO'D WANT TO SEE LITTLE MISS FLAT BUTT'S PANTIES ANYWAY?

OKAY.

I AWAIT YOUR QUESTIONS, RESPONSES, AND LETTERS!

I CAN EVEN CONSULT WITH THE ORIGINAL AUTHOR NISHINO-SENSEI...OR NOT! I CAN RESPOND HOWEVER I WANT!

ONCE I HAVE PANTIES, I'LL SHOW THEM TO YOU.

WE'RE GOING TO BUY YOU SOME UNDERWEAR!

SO IT'S A MOOT POINT.

I NEVER WEAR PANTIES ANYWAY.

All right, see you in Volume 5!

ANSWER: IN MY MIND, SHE DOESN'T WEAR PANTIES, SO EVEN THOUGH SHE'S HAD SEVERAL CHANCES FOR PANTY SHOTS, IF SHE'S NOT WEARING ANY... I CAN'T BRING MYSELF TO DRAW IT. (FYI: SHE WEARS PANTIES IN THE LIGHT NOVELS.)

STAFF CREDITS

translation	**Ryan Peterson**
adaptation	**Shannon Fay**
lettering/layout	**Ma. Victoria Robado**
cover design	**Nicky Lim**
proofreader	**Rebecca Scoble**
editor	**Adam Arnold**
publisher	**Jason DeAngelis**
	Seven Seas Entertainment

KANOKON OMNIBUS 3-4
Copyright © 2007-2008 Rin Yamaki, Katsumi Nishino / MEDIA FACTORY
First published in Japan in 2007-2008 by MEDIA FACTORY, Inc.
English translation rights reserved by Seven Seas Entertainment, LLC.
under the license from MEDIA FACTORY, Inc., Tokyo, Japan.

ISBN: 978-1-937867-36-2

Printed in Canada

First Printing: August 2013

10 9 8 7 6 5 4 3 2 1

FOLLOW US ONLINE: www.gomanga.com

READING DIRECTIONS

This book reads from *right to left*, Japanese style.
If this is your first time reading manga, you start
reading from the top right panel on each page and
take it from there. If you get lost, just follow the
numbered diagram here. It may seem backwards
at first, but you'll get the hang of it! Have fun!!